MEG'S CASTLE

MEG'S CASTLE

by Helen Nicoll
and Jan Pieńkowski

PUFFIN BOOKS

Meg, Mog and Owl
went to stay in a castle

They climbed up the spiral stairs

and
got into
a four poster bed

In the night

they heard weird noises

Meg made a spell

Send it away
Helmet and shield
And 6 foot spear
Ghastly ghost
Please disappear

The ghost vanished

A white knight appeared

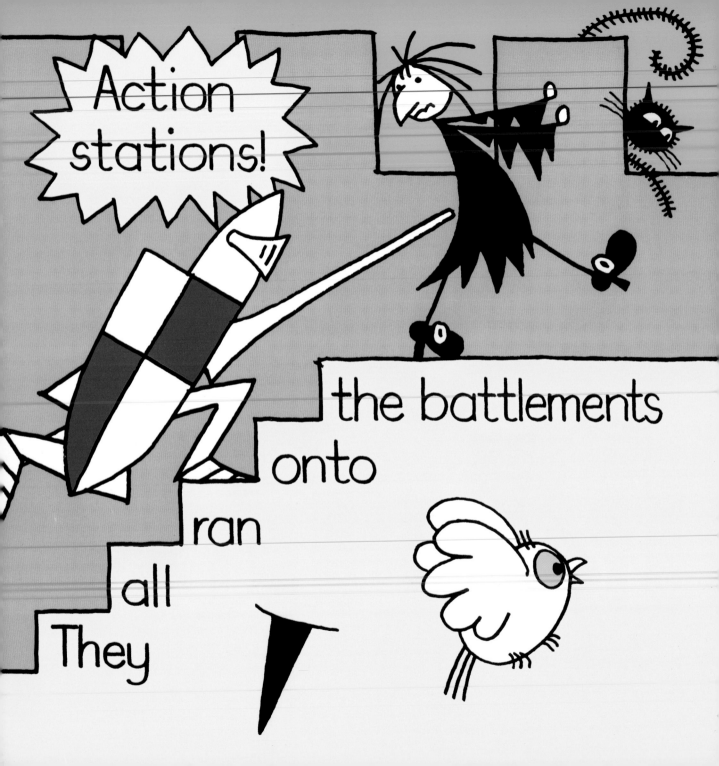

CHARGE

A green knight appeared

Owl
lowered

the
portcullis

Mog shot an arrow

and

poured

it

over

the

battlements

SPLASH

Owl
heaved
rocks
over
the
edge

The
green
knight
ran
away

They
had
a
feast
to
celebrate

After
the
feast
Meg
Mog
and
Owl
flew
home

Goodbye!